Rose's Betrayal and Survival

Phyllis A. Collmann

For additional copies of this or other
books written by Phyllis Collmann:
phyllisacollmann@hotmail.com
1-712-540-4082
www.collmannwarehouse.com

First printing 2002
Second printing 2005
Third printing 2008
Fourth printing 2013
Fifth printing 2016

Library of Congress Control Number: 2005905168

ISBN: 1-57579-313-X

Printed in the United States of America
Pine Hill Press
4000 West 57th Street
Sioux Falls, SD 57106

Dedication

To my husband Colin, for 53 years of marriage
And for his love and support.

To my children
whom I love very much.

∽ About the Author ∾

Phyllis A. Collmann is a retired nurse. She lives on a farm with her husband of 53 years. This is the first pioneer book in a series about Rose Donlin. The second book is called *Rose's Triumpant Return*. And the third book is called *Rose's Heart's Decision*.

Published Books:

Rose's Betrayal and Survival
Rose's Triumphant Return
Rose's Heart's Decision
Kim's Unplanned Saga
Mother's Innocence Proven

Chapter 1

Rose was packing. She was packing everything she owned. The telegram lay on her night stand. Her father had given it to her to read. It stated that she was going to Oklahoma.

The day before Rose's father, Louis Donlin, had hitched up his horses and made his spring trip into St. Louis. He had taken the furs he had trapped along the river to trade for his food supplies and purchase a few more traps. The town was located near the river, so it was only a short trip.

He was always home by late afternoon. While Louis Donlin had been picking up supplies in the general store, he had read a notice on the wall, which had stated that a man in Oklahoma wanted a bride, and was willing to pay for her.

Louis had thought about his daughter, Rose. If this man could pay for her, he must have money. Louis had sent a return telegram saying that he had a daughter to offer in marriage, and that he would take no less then fifty dollars. Rose Donlin was sold just like that.

Louis arrived home the next day with his supplies, a wooden box, and fifty dollars in his pocket. Rose was never told of the money exchange. To keep his secret, Louis had torn off the bottom half of the telegram.

Rose stood in her room, looking at the things that meant everything to her. She looked at the rag dolls her mother had made for her, and the patch quilt that covered her bed. How could her father make her leave her home?

Her books—she had so many. The wooden box sat on her bed, and Rose was placing all her books carefully in the box so that she would have room for all of them. She would not leave even one behind. The chances of her returning were next to none.

Since her mother had died, Rose had spent all of her time reading and learning. Her father had left her alone a lot. He was not the same since his wife's death and spent most of his time checking his traps. Before Rose's mother died, her father would take her along. During this time, he taught her about guns, how to skin animals, and how to stretch their hides. When Louis returned from checking his traps, Rose was packed and ready.

It was at this time he told her of the man in Oklahoma waiting to marry her. Rose Donlin stood in shocked amazement. To think she was being forced to marry someone named Joseph, who she had never met. Rose wanted to scream at her father, "I don't want to go!" Without one word, she turned and picked up her satchel. Her father picked up her box of books and put them in the wagon. The horses moved in their usual pace on the way to the railroad station. Rose and her father did not speak. Rose felt confused and afraid.

"I'm sorry, Rose, but this is for the best," her father said, as Rose stepped up onto the train. From St. Louis to Oklahoma would take two days, including all of the stops. Rose spent this time reading and thinking about what was ahead for her. Rose had never been disobedient, but the thought of getting off the train and going away on her own crossed her mind. She also knew that she could never disobey her father.

When the train came to a stop, all of the passengers hurriedly stood up and left the train. Rose stepped down and looked around. Everyone was leaving. Suddenly, she looked up, and a young man was walking toward her. She had never seen a man look like him. Rose then remembered, that she had seen someone similar in the Sears and Roebuck Company catalogue.

John Fitzpatrick had never seen a more beautiful girl as Rose. Her blond hair hung loosely to her shoulders. He looked directly into the prettiest blue eyes he had ever seen.

"Rose Donlin, are you Rose?" he asked.

She didn't answer. Her thoughts were on how she must look to him. Her mother had made the coat she had on five years ago. It covered her completely. "I'm making it big, Rose, so you can wear it a long time," her mother had said. The coat covered the worn-out dress she was wearing. It was the best she had. After her mother had died, her father did not care at all about her clothes.

"Rose?" John repeated.

"Yes, yes. I'm Rose," she answered.

"My name is John Fitzpatrick. I'm the bank president and a friend of Joseph Higgins. He asked me to pick you up and take you to his cabin."

"This could have been wonderful," she said to herself, trying to hide her disappointment.

John loaded her satchel and her box of books in the buggy. He mentioned to her how he loved to read, too. John tried to talk to her on the trip. He told her, "Joseph owns three thousand acres of land," but Rose's own thoughts kept her silent. The trip to Joseph Higgins' cabin took an hour.

It had been dry in the area for a long time, so the wheels of the buggy kicked up a lot of dust. Rose noticed that the soil had reddish color to it; she had never seen soil look like this. The land was flat, unlike

the rolling hills of Missouri, where she had come from.

Rose thought the weeds and brush even looked dry, and some tumbleweeds blew across the trail as the horses kept up their steady gait. Rose had seen only two farmsteads on the trip from town. She missed seeing the many trees that surrounded her home. She thought the country was so desolate, and suddenly she felt very lonely and homesick. She had never been this far from home before.

John pulled the horse to a stop in front of the cabin. No one came out. John stepped down, helped Rose down, and then unloaded her belongings. Rose was trembling as she slowly walked up to the cabin. She had to step over weeds and twigs. John reached over and took hold of her arm so that she would not trip on the broken step. John stood beside her at the door. He leaned over and said, "Please take care of yourself. If you need help, I'm always at the bank."

The door slowly opened, and a pale old man looked at her for a long time before he said, "Don't just stand there, come in." Inside the cabin, Rose stood in disbelief. It was so dark and dirty. John carried in her satchel and books. He noticed that she would have her own bedroom, as Joseph's bed was next to the fireplace.

"Joseph, this is Rose, from Missouri."

"Yah, yah," was Joseph's reply.

John left, and Joseph insisted Rose shut the door. The air in the cabin was heavy and stale. Rose felt weak, her heart was pounding, and she could hardly breathe. She needed to sit down. She reached out and grabbed the nearest chair. The chair she found was not only broken, but extremely dirty.

The table in the center of the room had a thick layer of dust on top of it. It was covered with dirty dishes. The food left on them was dry and hard. Rose knew that when it was dark, the rats and mice ate from them, too. The table was covered with their droppings. The fireplace had ashes falling out on the floor, and fumes caught in her throat, which made her feel like she was choking. The boards on the cabin floor had large cracks in them, which were filled with dirt.

Along the wall, next to the fireplace, were shelves. On one shelf stood a rusty cast-iron skillet. Next to the skillet were some dirty dishes and a few pieces of flatware. Next to the food-stained flatware stood a dark-stained coffee pot. Directly over the flames in the fireplace hung a cast-iron pot with the remains of soup in the bottom. Rose could see mold growing around the edge.

Rose sat for a long time remembering her home in Missouri, which had always been clean and well cared for. Since the death of her mother, Rose had begun to keep the pantry full.

Joseph had gotten back into bed with all of his clothes on, including his boots, and covered himself up. He was talking to himself. "I have always helped others, but now I'm unable to take care of myself. I paid for an older woman to take of me." His voice sounded angry. Rose did not hear what he said.

Joseph told Rose in a loud voice, "You will have to do chores, feed and water the horses and the chickens, gather the eggs, feed and water the cow and milk her. Follow the path to the creek to get water." Rose heard every word. Rose stood up and headed for the door to do his chores.

When Rose left the cabin, she noticed the small building behind the cabin. The roof needed repairs, so she was sure that it leaked. It also was leaning from the winds over the years. Rose thought it didn't look like the one that had belonged to her family in Missouri. Her father repaired it as needed. The door looked like it could fall off, because it was held on with only one hinge. This was, of course, the outhouse, and Rose needed to use it. She walked up to it slowly, opening the door carefully, and she knew immediately-without a doubt-that it had not been moved for a very long time.

The wiping paper was a Sears and Roebuck Company catalogue. It looked like the mice were using it, too, and little bits of paper lay all over the floor. She sat only a few minutes, for the seat was cold. Rose was right about the roof leaking. She could look up at the sky from any place inside. The hook, on the inside to hold the door shut, was gone. Holding the door shut, sitting on the seat, and all the rest was not easy. Rose would have to repair the outhouse. Rose wondered how Joseph made it outside to use it, as weak as he was.

All the water had to be carried up from the creek. On her way, she heard the horses whinnying for something to eat. Rose was surprised to see how well-kept they were, which told her that Joseph had struggled every day to feed and water them. After that, he had no energy to eat and bathe himself. Rose also noticed the liniment and salve, which he had used to take good care of his horses.

No one but Joseph had ever milked the cow. "The cow will stand anywhere in the barnyard to be milked," Joseph had said. Rose walked up to her and put the milking stool down. She set the pail on the ground. The old cow turned her head and looked directly at Rose. "Squeeze and pull, squeeze and pull," Joseph had instructed her. Without any warning, the old cow kicked, the pail tipped over, and what little milk there was spilled. Rose found herself sitting with her legs up in the air, and the stool was nowhere in sight. Making friends with that old cow was going to take time.

Rose had not been around chickens because since she had been raised along the river, predatory animals would come close to the house. Rose's father had always told her that the hens would be eaten faster than they could lay eggs. "Gather all the eggs. The hens have nests in the corral barn and hatching shed." Rose tried to act like she understood what Joseph was saying. What he didn't tell her was to be careful of that big old rooster, so she found it out by herself.

Rose walked into the corral first, and she wondered if the rustling of her dress scared the hens and the big old rooster, for they all squawked and flew in different directions.

Rose carried her basket like Joseph had told her, reached into the nests, gathered up the eggs, and put them in the basket. While her back was turned, that big rooster jumped in the air and scratched her back with his long spurs. Rose decided that this would never happen again.

Rose went down to the creek to carry enough water to heat for Joseph's bath, assuming that she could get him to take one. On entering the cabin, Rose would smell the body odor coming from Joseph, even while he was under the covers. His hair was long, full of snarls and unkempt. The smell was nauseating. His ears had hair and fuzz in them. Joseph had scaly areas around his forehead. His face was dirty, and he had not shaved for a long time. His fingernails had dirt under them and needed to be cut. His eyes had matter in them, and Rose wondered how he could see.

Rose didn't want to know how long Joseph had been wearing the clothes he had on. She was going to have to soak them a long time before they would be clean again. Rose heated the water for his bath. She poured water into his basin, and laid his towel, wash rag, and lye soap beside it. "I'm going to the creek, Joseph, to wash clothes, while you take your bath," Rose told him. The look Joseph gave her made her unsure what he was going to do.

Chapter 2

The area in which Rose chose to do Joseph's wash was the place where he always tied his canoe. Rose looked it all over. The canoe looked like it was in good condition. She was sure it had not been used recently; the only wet spot on it was the end that sat in the water. Rose was seriously considering escaping in the canoe. She knew how to row. Even if the canoe would tip over, or if it would leak, she was an excellent swimmer. She would row as fast as she could. Which direction of the creek should she go?

Her thoughts were racing. She wanted to escape. But what about Joseph? He was an old man who was very sick. Who would take care of him? A feeling of unhappiness and uncertainty came over her. Rose finally put the idea of escaping out of her mind.

When Rose finished washing his clothes in the creek, she hung them on the porch railing to dry overnight. Rose found that Joseph had given himself a bath and put on the only clean clothes he had. It took convincing, but Rose talked Joseph into letting her shave him and cut his hair. She was very careful about the open areas on his head and neck, and she was sure that rats had been chewing on him at night. Rose knew exactly what she was going to put on them. She ran to the barn to get that salve she had seen earlier. She spread it on generously.

When Rose had finished, Joseph mentioned he had not eaten all day. Rose would not eat one bit of food until every cast-iron skillet was clean. She carried all the pots and flatware to the creek, soaked them, and scrubbed them with a bar of lye soap. After each piece was washed, she laid it on the grass beside the bank to dry off.

Rose thought cleaning the cabin would take her a long time because there was no doubt that it had taken many years of not being cleaned to look as badly as it did. Spiders were hanging in webs in all the corners of the cabin. None of the windows had curtains on them, except one that had only one-half a curtain, which was shredded and torn. The chimney on the lamp was black, and when Rose lit the lamp, it gave out hardly any light at all. She very carefully removed the chimney and cleaned it. The lamp was the only one in the cabin.

ᴄᴏ Chapter 3 ᴇᴏ

The fireplace had to be cleaned, for the evenings and nights were turning cold, as winter was approaching. The ashes were almost up to the bottom of the cast-iron skillet. Rose found an old pan, which she used as a scoop to dig out the ashes and dump them in a pail. The black dust filled the air, and she noticed her hands and dress were black.

Joseph yelled at her. "Open the door, I can't breathe, and leave it open until you finish." Rose wanted to yell back at him but didn't. When Rose finished cleaning the fireplace, she walked into her bedroom to see it before it was dark, because she did not have a lamp in her room.

The room was small. The only furniture was her bed, one chair, and an old trunk. The walls showed all the two-by-fours. The boards on which the cabin was built were nailed on to the two-by-fours. The room had no closet. Rose hung up her few clothes on the large nails that were pounded into the boards.

The room had only one small window. The frame and window were not straight. It was lower on one side. The glass was cracked. It had no curtain and probably never had one.

The ceiling of the room was the rafters. The floor had several holes leading under the cabin. Rose knew that she had to close up the holes, because they were large enough for rodents or snakes to enter. Rose closed her eyes for a minute and remembered the bedroom she had been forced to leave in Missouri. The walls were nice and smooth, curtains hung on the windows, and she had rugs on the floor that her mother had made from scraps of material. Little tears squeezed out of her eyes and ran down her cheeks.

Rose prepared Joseph's supper. It consisted of the only thing they had- eggs. After they had eaten, Joseph asked Rose if she would read to him. He went to sleep while she was still reading. Rose closed the book, took care of the fireplace, and walked softly to her room. She was wondering how her father could have done this. Rose cried herself to sleep.

The next morning, she awoke and threw her covers off. Rose started to put her feet on the floor, but she quickly pulled her

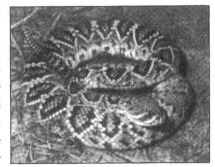

feet back up on the bed. Rose knew immediately what that sound was: a rattlesnake lay next to her boots.

Her father had warned her many times to be extremely careful, if she heard this noise. "Stand perfectly still and slowly turn your head to the direction the noise is coming from," he had said. "You must never make sudden moves because this is when they strike, and their venom is very poisonous." Rose remembered her father's words.

Rose inched her body to the opposite side of the bed. She pulled up one of her blankets to throw over the snake. As she raised her blanket and looked over the edge of her bed, the snake was gone. The snake was hiding somewhere in her bedroom.

Rose wondered if the snake was as frightened as she was. Rose reached down and grabbed her boots, turned them up side down, and shook them fiercely while sitting with her feet up on her bed. She leaned over to reach her clothes that were lying on the chair. She lifted them carefully, dressed, and left her bed unmade. She would need to shake all of her blankets before getting back into bed that night.

Rose left her bedroom making sure she closed the door. She didn't want the snake out by Joseph. Rose told Joseph about the snake in her bedroom.

"Rose, you have to catch it and get it out of the cabin before you go to bed tonight. Find the snake before it finds you. You need a strong stick," he told her. After Rose found a stick, she went back into her bedroom, knowing that she had to find the rattlesnake. Hoping to hear the scary sound of the rattle, Rose tapped on the walls and slowly inched her way around the room. She carried the stick in one hand and held a blanket in the other. It took a while before she heard the sound of the snake. Rose needed the

Rose's Betrayal and Survival

snake to come completely out of its hiding place. It slithered out toward her. When she saw the snake coil and get ready to strike, she was so frightened. She quickly threw the blanket over it. Rose picked up the edges of the blanket and swiftly headed out the door.

"Make sure the snake is dead, because you need to skin it and put the meat in the smokehouse." Joseph yelled at her. Rose beat the blanket with every ounce of strength she had. Carefully she lifted the blanket with the stick. The snake was almost dead, but she needed to make sure. She ran as fast as she could and got the axe. Rose chopped off the head, dug a hole and buried it. After the dreaded fear of catching the snake and killing it subsided, Rose wondered how Joseph could have asked her to skin the snake or how he expected her to cook it and eat the meat.

Chapter 4

All the chores were still waiting for her. Rose fed and watered the horses first, then she milked the cow. It was getting easier. She took care of the chickens, including gathering the eggs. She heard the big old rooster in flight behind her. Quickly turning, she moved back, and lifted her dress. Her leg sent him upside-down on the barn floor. He staggered to his feet, shook his head, ruffled his feathers, and wandered off. The rooster would test her at different times, but Rose was always watching him.

Rose was busy learning about Joseph: doing his chores, carrying water from the creek to the cabin for cooking and dishes, and trying to find enough food for them to eat.

When he mentioned one more chore she had to do, he began by telling her, "You will need to turn the cow chips today." Rose repeated what she thought she had heard him say, not understanding one word of what he had said. Joseph continued, "Tomorrow evening, they should be dry. Pick them up and store them in the wood shed. They will be ready to burn this winter."

"Cow chips," Rose said. "Burn them where this winter?" Joseph turned his head and looked the other way. He could tell exactly what Rose was thinking. She had never heard about cow chips.

After the chores were done, Rose walked toward the food cellar, hoping she would find some food good enough to eat. She pulled and tugged, and the whole door landed on top of her, knocking her to the ground. Rose crawled out from under it and peered down into the cave. Taking one step at a time, she went down the steps until she was standing on the floor of the cave. Rose was standing in a black, gooey liquid that was all over her boots.

Rose examined the food on the shelves. It was rotten and smelled bad. Apparently Joseph had not raised a garden for many years. Rose wondered if he would let her go into town and get supplies. They would surely starve with winter coming.

Maybe she could go to the bank. No, she couldn't do that, because her dress was all torn and faded. This dress was the only one she had. Rose walked to the creek and cleaned the black, gooey liquid off of her boots. The cold water was so hard on her hands that they were becoming chapped and red.

Joseph was awake when she returned to the cabin. Rose told Joseph to get ready for breakfast. He sat and looked at her, and she finally said, "Joseph, wash your face and hands." He ate his breakfast of scrambled eggs made with fresh milk and eggs. Joseph had not tasted anything as good for a long time.

Rose mentioned the trip into town for supplies. "I'll go tomorrow," Joseph abruptly replied. She tried to tell him that she should go, too. "Joseph, you are not well enough to go alone."

He firmly said, "No!"

Joseph spent the day resting, while Rose cleaned and repaired the cave. Rose could not understand why she could not get the cellar floor clean. The black gooey liquid just kept seeping in. Finally, she put boards down so that she could walk on the floor.

⮜ Chapter 5 ⮞

When Rose returned to the cabin, she made a list of supplies needed for cooking and baking. At the bottom she wrote. "Tar paper and boards to fix the holes in the cabin." Traps were needed for the rats and snakes, which Rose feared the most. She also asked for seeds for a garden that she planned to raise. The seeds would store until spring. A milk pail was needed because the old pail was full of rust. Rose did not know when Joseph would make the next trip.

That night, Joseph lay down and again asked if Rose would read to him. When Rose thought he was sleeping, she walked to her room. She crawled into bed and began to cry. She knew if her mother were alive, she would not have been sent here. Rose had always tried so hard to please her father but he had made the decision to send her here.

Early the next morning, Rose fed Joseph breakfast. Then, she went to the corral and harnessed the horses exactly the way her father had taught her to. She backed them up, hitched them to the wagon, and drove the team up along side the porch. With her help, Joseph only had to climb upon the buckboard. Rose covered him with a large blanket, led the team onto the trail, and stepped aside.

Rose stood and watched until Joseph was completely out of sight. She hurried back into the cabin and went directly to Joseph's dirty bed. She tore the covers off and pulled the straw mattress across the floor to the door. She placed it up over the porch railing, found an old limb, and proceeded to beat it firmly.

Rose went back to clean under his bed. She pulled out a wooden box. Opening the box, she found many guns that were in good condition. Rose decided a take a loaded revolver to keep in her room. She hoped that Joseph would not notice.

She pulled out a small box. It contained his personal papers. The deed to his land rested on top. A banker was taking care of the many acres rented by other farmers. Rose was overwhelmed by the amount of cash that lay in the bottom of the box. Rose now knew that Joseph was a very, very wealthy man. She also knew that no amount of money would ever get her to marry him.

Chapter 6

She cleaned up the dirt and rat droppings, and went down to the creek. Rose tore off her clothes and swam out as far as she could. The water was cold, but she didn't even notice. Her ability to survive what her father had gotten her into was all she could think of.

It was at this time when she swam around the bend in the creek, she found a small secluded inlet. The branches hung over the calm, clear, blue, water, making it very private. This is where Rose would go to be alone. She could slip into the water and not be seen.

There was absolutely nothing here to eat until she walked by the corral. The chickens were all out, eating and scratching. Within the hour, Joseph had one less chicken. It was in the cast-iron cooking pot over the flame in the fireplace. She prayed silently, thanking her father for teaching her how to skin animals.

Supper was ready when Joseph pulled the team up to the porch. Rose went out and tied the team to the railing. Then, carefully, she helped him down. She helped him into the cabin and took off his old worn-out hat, tattered coat, and boots. She sat him on his clean bed. Rose fed him his supper.

After he had finished eating, she gently placed him on his bed and covered him with the blankets that she had warmed next to the fireplace earlier. Rose had always had an enormous curiosity. She questioned Joseph about what was happening in town. She hoped he would mention John Fitzpatrick, but he didn't.

The horses were still tied to the railing of the porch, so she knew what was expected of her. The flour, sugar, beans, corn, and wheat came in fifty-pound bags. Rose dragged them into the cabin and left them just inside the door. In the morning, she would empty the flour into the flour bin. The sugar, beans, corn, and wheat would be stored in tin cans. Rose had learned from her mother to take the thread out of the bags, wash them, and use them for dish towels and aprons. She would grind the corn and wheat to make their bread each day.

Rose lit the lantern and led the horses around behind the cabin to the smokehouse. She wondered how she could get the slab of meat up and hung onto the hooks hanging from the ceiling. She tied a rope around the quarter of beef, swung the rope over the hook, and pulled the smoked meat up over the hook. Rose got the meat hung and locked the door so that no animals could get in. Rose led the horses to the food cellar. She unloaded the potatoes, lard, and vegetables. The horses were then led to the shed, next to the corral, to unload the burlap bags full of grain. Rose drove the team back up to the cabin. Joseph had not forgotten anything. She laid one board at a time next to the side of the cabin, along with the tar paper. There was something else in the wagon. Using the lantern, she found a box of books—the most wonderful thing he could have given her. There was also a ready-made dress and pair of boys' work boots. Rose had not expected Joseph to bring her anything.

Rose led the horses to the corral. She unhitched them, hung up the harnesses, turned the horses loose, and fed them. They drank water from the small tank that she filled each day from the creek.

She headed toward the cabin with her belongings. She surveyed each book before going to sleep. The weather seemed unpredictable. When Rose went out in the morning, it was very cold. The creek had a thin layer of ice on it. Rose explained to Joseph at breakfast that she could not get any water. "The axe was made to chop things. That means wood and ice. Find a place where the bank is sheltered and the ice will not be so thick," Joseph sternly told her. "Gather the eggs early in the mornings when you go out to do chores. Go a couple of times before supper. That way, the eggs will not freeze. Nothing must go to waste," Joseph ordered.

The holes in the cabin had to be fixed. The cold air was coming in all over. Rose was burning more wood and the supply was quickly diminishing. Rose had to open her bedroom door at night to allow the warmth from the fireplace to enter. Her room was extremely cold. She was more afraid of freezing than she was of Joseph.

The cabin could not look any worse. The boards were cracked and warped, so whatever Rose did to fix it up was okay in her mind. Rose rolled the tar paper out and started at one corner. She tacked it up and went completely around the cabin, nailing it as she went. While doing this, she thought there was enough tar paper to cover the bottom with two layers. She would make sure that a rat would not chew on her head. With half the cabin covered in tar paper, Rose had time to nail only a few boards around the bottom. The afternoon was gone. It was time to do chores and make supper. Tomorrow, Rose would work on the cabin again.

Rose went into the cabin to build the fire and to get warm. Her hands were so cold that she could hardly stand it. Joseph noticed, and he offered her his rawhide gloves, which she accepted. When Rose had finished her chores, it was completely dark. She took the lantern down into the food cellar and got potatoes and enough lard to make biscuits for supper and breakfast. Rose then went to the smoke-house and cut off meat for supper.

Supper was soon over and Rose was exhausted. All she could think of was laying her head on her pillow. "Would you read one of your new books to me?" she heard Joseph ask. Rose wondered who would fall asleep first.

Chapter 7

Rose woke just as the sun was beginning to shine in her window. Her first thought was all the work she needed to get done that day. She hoped that Joseph would let her open the door to the cabin today to let in some fresh air, since the air in the cabin was always so stale. Opening the widows would not work for two reasons: Joseph allowed no breeze on him, and the windows in the cabin were built so that they did not open at all.

Rose made Joseph his breakfast. She tried to do her chores earlier, because she needed to get to the creek to wash clothes. Her mind was busy thinking of ways to help Joseph feel better. The splashing of the water while she scrubbed the clothes blocked out any noise. A feeling came over her, and little shivers shook her body. Rose heard something; she stopped rinsing Joseph's overalls. A frightening horror was coming toward her. She determined at that second she was going to die.

A large brown bear stopped and stood up on his back feet, and then opened his large mouth. This was the largest, most vicious-looking creature she had ever read about. She had read that brown bears love to chase, and so she knew that she could not run.

Quickly but quietly, she moved into the water. Rose had been a tiny little girl when she first learned to swim. In the water, she was never afraid. She could hear the bear coming fast. Rose submerged to the bottom and swam underwater as long as she could hold her breath. She came to the surface without splashing because she did not know where the bear was. He was nowhere in sight. Rose looked around and did not see it.

The first noise Rose heard was a heavy breathing sound, followed by a mean growl. Her clothes were dripping and felt heavy. Her first instinct was to hide, but when she turned her head the bear was already coming. The barn and corral were the closest build-ings, but then the horses, cow, and chickens would be

his spoil. Rose knew she could not get to the cabin before the bear overtook her. The only building she could possibly reach was the outhouse.

As she stepped in, her hand grabbed the door and pulled it upright. The door was sagging with the one hinge. She held onto it while bracing herself. Within two minutes, the bear was there. He sounded out of breath. He was making all sorts of cruel noises. This savage beast was not going to give up. Rose had read many stories about bears. She knew he would not eat her, but could tear her body apart.

The bear stood up on his back legs and put his weight against the outhouse. His claws were pushing and scratching on the boards over her head. The building began to squeak, and vibrate with his weight. If he tipped it over, she had no chance at all to survive.

Her body was frozen with fear. Her hands felt numb, and they were red from holding the door closed. Suddenly Rose heard the terrible sound of wood cracking, and the bear's paw broke a board. His paw, with large long black claws, was within inches of her arm.

He pulled his paw back. She heard a different sound coming from him. It was as if he were moaning. Rose looked toward the opening that the bear had made with his paw. On a board sticking up was blood. He had cut his paw open on the old and petrified boards.

Rose remained in the outhouse for some time, peeking out of the opening. When she calmed down and worked up enough nerve, she opened the door slowly. One foot at a time, she stepped out. The first thing she noticed was a small trail of blood leading away from Joseph's homestead.

After Rose told Joseph about the brown bear, he was adamant that she learn to use a gun. Rose wanted to tell him that she knew already, but couldn't. Joseph explained, "The bear could have wandered out of the Colorado mountains and probably was trying to find his way back." Joseph hoped that they would never see it again. Rose knew she would carry the memory of the bear for the rest of her life.

Chapter 8

Joseph was sitting at the table in front of the fireplace. "I washed my face and hands," Joseph said, with a smile on his face. Rose smiled to herself. She thought she would work on getting something done about his teeth and fingernails.

Instead of getting back into bed, Joseph sat at the table while Rose read to him. She read about Columbus' voyage. Rose new he had heard the story many times before, but enjoyed hearing it again. It had been many years since Joseph attended school. He was a well-educated man. After she stopped reading. Rose tried to get him to tell her about his life. He got up slowly and crawled into bed without a word.

The afternoon warmed up enough so that Rose could work on the cabin. Joseph had gotten the right amount of tarpaper and boards so that the cabin could be completely covered. Rose's hands, arms, and shoulders were so sore that the horse liniment was the only relief she could find.

The winter was very cold. The water pail in the cabin was frozen each morning. Rose sat the water pail close to the fire to thaw out. She always placed it back on the water stand, so that it would stay cold for Joseph. He insisted on having a glass of water with each meal.

The ice on the creek was getting thicker. Carrying water was becoming extremely difficult. Rose would lead one horse at a time to the spot she had chopped open to drink. She managed to carry enough water for the cow, the chickens, and for Joseph to wash himself. Joseph would mutter or grumble when she made him bathe and change his clothes. She just pretended not to hear him.

Covering the cabin had stopped any more rats or snakes from coming in. The traps had caught the ones already inside. "I can survive now," Rose thought. When Rose had first arrived at the cabin, she had begun marking the days off on a piece of paper. Rose knew that on March fifteenth, she would be eighteen years old. She knew that the year was 1880.

One early spring morning, the skys were dark. The wind was strong and bitterly cold. "It looks like a late winter blizzard coming," Joseph said. Rose worked the whole day. She cared for the animals and then locked them in the barn. She brought in extra food from the food cellar and meat from the smokehouse. The snow began to fall. It stung her face because the wind was so fierce. Rose knew that she would have to stay up to keep the fire going. It would be so easy for them to freeze if the fire went out.

Joseph lay in his bed that night while she read to him. Then, he gradually told her why he came to live there. His father had sent for him, because his mother was very ill and needed to be cared for. "I was working at the bank in town. I left my job and moved here. My mother died after a few years, and then my father was no longer able to work. I decided just to stay," he confided.

While Joseph talked, Rose compared her life to his. Was she doomed to stay here, and would she end up old with no one to care for her? Rose lay in bed that night and her thoughts were about John Fitzpatrick. If only she would have been sent to marry John, everything would have turned out so differently.

The storm left Rose with a lot of work. It took several tries to open the cabin door. The snow was so deep, and the wind was also blowing making it difficult to see. "The scoop is hanging on the back of the smokehouse," Joseph hollered. To get to the barn, Rose had to scoop a path through the snow bank that had drifted in, from the cabin to the barn door.

The animals were all fine. Rose fed them and then struggled to get to the creek. She went to the sheltered area where she had always gotten water before. She filled her pail. She made many trips, because the animals had gone without water during the storm.

When the chores were done, Rose was exhausted. But she was also relieved that all of Joseph's livestock had made it safely through the storm. The storm had come and passed. Winter had finally given up.

Chapter 9

In the spring of 1881, they heard a loud, shrill cry. "It's a mountain cat!" Joseph shouted at Rose. She was up and dressed in no time. Joseph was on his knees pulling the box of guns out from under his bed when Rose got to him. He handed her the shotgun and said, "Load it." He proceeded to tell her what to do, "Run to the corral and lock up the horses. Lock the cow and chickens in the barn. That's what the big cat will be after." While Rose put on her coat, Joseph lit the lantern for her. Rose ran and did exactly what Joseph had told her.

When the animals were safely locked up, Rose walked about twenty feet from the corral. She shot into the air, reloaded, walked a little further, and shot into the air again to scare the cat into thinking he was being shot at.

After returning to the cabin, Rose asked Joseph why he thought she knew how to load a gun. "When you take a man's revolver and ammunition, it's for sure the person who took it knows about guns," he explained. Rose did not answer.

The next morning, Rose found the cat's tracks very close to the cabin. "The cat followed the creek and smelled the animals. He was not going to leave," Joseph told her. The next few nights Rose locked up all the animals before coming into the cabin—especially the horses, which were the most valuable. Joseph handed Rose a rifle, saying, "Rabbit is the best bait for a trap."

The trap was hanging in the barn, and it had been quite some time since it was used last. Joseph ordered, "Bring the trap to the cabin and I will help you set it." Rose could hardly carry the trap, it was so heavy.

Joseph came out on the porch to help open the jaws of the trap and set it. It took both of them to get it set.

Rose lugged the trap down to the area where she had seen the big cat's tracks. To keep the cat from dragging the trap away, Joseph told her to drive a stake through the largest link of the chain attached to the trap. Rose found a large hammer in the barn, and after some strenuous pounding, the trap was secure.

While hunting rabbits for bait, Rose discovered something as she walked along a brush-covered area. There were several pools of the black gooey liquid, just like she had seen on the floor of the food cellar. Rose stood for a few minutes watching it slowly bubbling. Small popping bubbles kept coming to the surface. She noticed the shiny color, and when she touched it, it felt cold and slippery. Rose remembered reading somewhere about the discovery of something they called crude oil. Rose wondered whether this was oil and why Joseph had not told her about it. Rose thought to herself that when the time was right, she would ask him about it.

When Rose had found that the cat had taken the rabbit, they realized how smart that old cat was, and how hard it was going to be to catch him. Rose's dress hung to her ankles, and as she walked, it caught on the weeds and brush. Rose tripped and fell several times, and the rifle she was carrying fell with her. When Rose got into a thick brush area, she tripped over a limb, and the rifle went off. Rose lay still for a long time, frightened and thankful that she had not been hit.

Rose struggled to her feet, lifted her skirt with one hand, and held the rifle with the other. Hunting rabbits with a dress on was very difficult. "I fell several times today. My dress caught on the brush and limbs. Joseph, I need a pair of your overalls," Rose explained.

Joseph didn't answer right away. Then he said, "I have never seen a girl in pants before."

Rose took a pair of his clean overalls out of his box. She went into her bedroom and slipped out of her dress. The overalls were too big for her. She tightened the straps and made a large cuff. Then she tied string around her waist and around the cuffs. The knock on her door was loud. Joseph said, "Come out and let me see you." Rose opened the door slowly and stepped out.

"Rose, you are wearing my pants and my shirt," Joseph laughed out loud.

Rose laughed too, and said, "It should be easier now."

When Rose set the trap this time, she did it like Joseph had told her to. He warned her many times not to get her hand or arm inside the jaws of the trap. "Take a stick and very slowly and carefully place the rabbit inside the jaws. Take the stick, tie another rabbit on the end and drag it all around the trap, so the cat will not smell you," Joseph instructed. "When you are done, take the rabbit and put it in the smoke-house, to save it for a meal for us," he continued.

On the way to do chores the next morning, Rose went to check the trap. That cat was even smarter than they had originally thought. He was eating very well these days, and then hiding somewhere by the creek. A better plan had to be devised. Joseph said, "Go to the cave and bring some lard. Set it next to the fireplace so it will melt while you go and hunt more rabbits."

Rose needed to get back with the rabbit early, because she had to skin the rabbit and drip its blood into the lard. She then had to pour the mixture on the inside of the trap and on the jaws of the trap. It would be very slippery. Rose carefully laid the skinned rabbit on the trap. Joseph warned her each time what would happen if it closed on her. As small as she was, it could take her arm right off.

The cry they heard in the early morning was one of pain. They got up quickly and dressed. Joseph handed Rose the rifle and said, "Through the heart, and don't get any closer than ten feet." He was right. Joseph was always right. The cat had one leg caught in the trap and nearly chewed it off.

Rose squatted, aimed the rifle, and pulled the trigger. The big cat lay dead. As Rose skinned the big cat, she noticed all the scars it had. This cat must have been older and hunting for easier prey. She stretched and hung the hide on the wall of the smokehouse. On the next trip to town, the hide would be sold.

Rose made up her mind. She would not eat the cat. She would eat the rabbits, but not the cat. Joseph explained to her that if they had not killed the cat, it would have chewed its leg completely off. It would have disappeared, healed, and come back with more determination than ever to get one of the horses.

⤳ Chapter 10 ⤲

The days were getting warmer. The ice on the creek was gone. It was easier to carry water now. Rose planned to make Joseph take baths again. She knew he would dislike it. Rose was aware that the supplies were getting low again, so she started a new list. She added a broom, paper to write on, and a cast-iron stove to cook on during the hot weather. The heat in the cabin from the fireplace would become unbearable.

Rose offered to go to town, and again, Joseph refused. The morning he was about to leave, two of the farmers who rented some of his land came up the road with a bull tied on the back of the buckboard. "Rose, get in the cabin and stay there with the door locked until I return," Joseph ordered.

Rose went into her room, sat in her chair, and cried until she fell asleep. There were only three people in the whole world who knew that she even existed. Despite how sad that made her feel, she was determined to survive.

In the late afternoon, Joseph pulled the wagon up outside the door. She helped him down and into the cabin. She fed him supper and helped him into bed. She really wanted to ask if he had seen John Fitzpatrick, but she didn't. Rose went out to unload the wagon. The food supplies needed to be unloaded first. She had to carry the smoked meat down into the food cellar because the summer heat would spoil it.

The black gooey liquid was up over the boards that Rose had laid on the floor last fall. Again, she carried more boards and laid them on top of the ones that were already there. Tonight, she would mention the oil to Joseph.

Rose backed the horses up till the buckboard was up to the smokehouse door. She unhitched the team and took the horses to the corral. She removed the harnesses, fed and watered the horses, and headed to the cabin.

Rose thought that if Joseph could rest tonight he would be able to help unload the new stove in the morning. While eating breakfast, Joseph told Rose how they would get the stove into the smokehouse. "Get two, good, sturdy boards and lay them in the wagon next to the stove. Let the ends stick out of the back of the wagon," Joseph continued. "We'll both get in the wagon and lift the stove up so the legs of the stove are on the boards, and slowly we'll push the stove to the edge. When the stove reaches the end of the wagon, the board will tip down, and we'll let the stove inch its way to the smokehouse floor."

It took all their strength to hold the stove so that it slid slowly down. When the stove was inside, Joseph said, "We'll finish tomorrow. The gunnysack in the wagon is yours." Rose now had writing paper, new books to read, a pair of overalls that fit.

The new stove was in the summer kitchen, as Rose called it. Joseph made a small opening into the cabin for Rose to carry food out to cook, and to come in and set it on the table. Rose hung a blanket over the opening to try and keep the heat out of the cabin.

Chapter 11

Joseph was now feeling stronger. He spent more time outside. Rose put a blanket on a chair and he sat in the summer sun. Rose sat on the ground, and Joseph told different stories about the land. He told about how his father had homesteaded the land. It was then Rose told Joseph about the black liquid in the cave, and the pools she found while hunting rabbits.

Joseph said with a firm voice, "It's been here a long time, and I'm not going to tell anyone. People would come and ruin my land. They would come with their big drilling machines and drive all over my land, digging it up. The cattle would not have green pastures to graze on." Rose wondered why the value of the oil did not interest him.

One morning while Rose was doing chores in the barn, she heard Joseph call her name. He shouted, "Stay in the barn! Do not come out." Joseph's renter was coming up the road with a load of wood. He was coming to take his bull home.

Rose stayed in the barn. She wanted to go right out and tell them she was here. Instead, she slipped quietly out the back door of the barn and walked to the creek where she would not be seen. She took off her shirt, new overalls, and boots. She slipped into the water and swam to her private inlet. Rose swam hard and fast, trying to relieve her feeling of being trapped. She slowly crawled out of the water.

The tall, black-haired man appeared out of nowhere. He wore only a pair of overalls. His body was smooth and dark brown from the sun. His chest and muscular arms showed signs of hard work. His steel blue eyes stared at Rose.

Taking her by surprise, he reached out and grabbed her shoulders. He lowered his hands to cup her breasts. He quickly moved his hands down to her hips. Continuing on, his hands moved inward. He knocked Rose to the ground. He was on top of her. He was trying to tear her underclothes off.

Rose was fighting for her life. The man was heavy and strong. She was squirming and wiggling. One of his hands was up under her undershirt groping at her breast. The other hand was ripping her bloomers. He moved a little to the side, and Rose pushed him as hard as she could.

Rose struggled to her feet. The man was up in front of her. They were staring at each other. Instantly, swiftly, she drew her arm back. Her hand made a fist, while her knee came up high, directly between his legs. Rose hit his nose and groin area at the same time.

The moan the man made was relief to Rose. It was excruciating pain for the man. He doubled over and fell to the ground. Rose's clothes were in her hands, and her feet were moving as fast as they could. She ran until she found the place she knew she could wade across the creek carrying her clothes over her head. Rose headed for the barn to dress. She felt temporarily disoriented. She hurried through her chores.

The man's image, scent, and the feel of his hands on her body were still on her mind. Rose decided to keep it a secret. She feared that Joseph would have the man hunted down, and perhaps killed. Only Rose knew the length Joseph would go to protect her and keep her only to himself.

After the renter had unloaded the wood in a huge pile next to the cabin, he tied his bull behind the wagon and headed home. Joseph was preparing for another winter with Rose. Rose felt that now she was Joseph's prisoner, and he would never let her go. She had no money and no clothes except for what she was wearing. At this time, she felt she could not go home to her father.

Rose went back to the cabin and didn't talk to Joseph the rest of the day. She decided that when he asked her to read that evening she was going to say, "No." The only lamp they had was sitting on the table. She knew that if she broke it while moving it into her room, she would never read at night again. So, she went into her room, closed the door, locked it with a lock she had found, crawled into bed, and cried herself to sleep.

∽ Chapter 12 ∾

The next morning, breakfast was eaten in silence. Then Joseph said, "It looks like we could have a wind storm. It's so hot and the wind is getting stronger. You need to lock up the animals, and close the barn doors so the wind will not tear them off."

Rose did everything he told her to do. She was busy carrying in food supplies when she noticed that the wind was getting stronger. Suddenly, the sky turned day into night. Joseph ordered Rose, "Go to the food cellar." He had been through storms like this before, and they were called tornadoes. She turned, looked at him, and said, "No, I'm not going without you." Rose helped Joseph outside.

When they got outside the cabin, the wind was so strong, that they had to hold on to each other. Branches, sticks, leaves, and dust were flying through the air. They could hardly get their breath. Huddling together, they made it to the cave door. It took both of them to get the door open. They started down into the dark cave holding the door so it wouldn't fly open. Rose held onto Joseph because she was so afraid he would fall. Pulling the door closed, they took one step at a time until they reached the bottom step. She told him, "Sit down."

They sat listening to the wind in silence. Then Joseph said, "I had forgotten how damp and cold it was down here." Rose moved closer to him, only to give him her body heat.

After nearly an hour, Rose went up the steps and opened the door. The storm was over. She went back to help Joseph. By that time, he was very cold. She almost carried him back to the cabin. Rose took off his coat, cap, and boots and put him under the covers. She immediately started the fireplace to warm him.

The storm left a mess for Rose to clean up. She discovered that the smokehouse roof had been torn completely off. She made all the repairs the best she could, then did her chores as usual. The following morning, another one of the tenant farmers came with a load of wood and to see if Joseph had made it through the storm.

Without a word, Rose went to her bedroom, closed the door, locked it, and began to write her life story. She started with the wonderful life she had had in St. Louis when her mother was alive. Her mother had taught her about love, kindness, and the strength to endure. She had also taught Rose to read and to love books. Rose wrote about her father, trying hard not to hate him.

The summer days were long for Rose. She tried to get along with Joseph. She tried to understand why he wanted no one to see her or anyone to know she was here. Rose knew this was not what she had planned for herself, but she was surprised at how strong she had become. Her spirit had not been broken.

Chapter 13

The knock on the cabin door was unexpected. Rose stopped cleaning the table, and went into her bedroom, shutting the door behind her. Joseph was taken by surprise when he opened the door, and two young children were standing there. He recognized them. They were children of one of his renters.

The boy looked to be about twelve years old. His face looked sad and old for his age. He wore no shoes. His overalls had holes in both knees. One shoulder strap was broken. He wore no shirt. His face, hands, and feet were caked with dirt.

Joseph guessed the girl to be around ten years old. Her hair was tangled with snarls. The dress she was wearing was ragged, torn, and looked too small for her. She too, was very dirty. She stood back behind her brother with her head down.

"Please, do not tell our father, he will be angry with us," the young boy told Joseph. Joseph reassured them he would never reveal anything to their father. They began by telling Joseph, "Father is very ill. Mother is doing the farm work." They went on to tell Joseph, "We have no money for food, and our father refuses to go to the doctor, so he stays ill."

Joseph felt sick to his stomach. Since he himself has been ill, this family could not come to him for help. He told the children, "Go home. I will come as soon as I can." Joseph stepped back into the cabin. He needed to tell Rose he would be gone for a couple of days. He needed to help this family. They had suffered long enough.

Joseph told Rose that he was going into town for medicine and food supplies for a renter, who was ill. Joseph carefully explained to Rose what he wanted her to do, "Do chores early in the morning. That way, you can be finished early in the evening. Always be in the cabin before dark. You must never go out after dark. The bolt on the door must be in place. Do not unbolt it for anyone. During the day stay close to the cabin, in case you need to hide in a hurry. The guns are all loaded in the gun box. Rose, you know how to use them. Use one if you have too." He paused, and said, "I need you to be safe in the cabin while I'm gone."

"I'll be safe Joseph, you take care of yourself," Rose answered.

Joseph arrived at the renter's farm and found him very ill. Joseph insisted he would go into town, explain the renter's condition to the doctor, and would bring him medicine and supplies. "I have no money at this time, and harvest is a month away," the renter told Joseph.

"You have nothing to worry about; you and your family come first." Joseph told him.

Joseph stopped at the bank and he told John Fitzpatrick about his renter. He told John that he was taking medicine and supplies to his renter. He also told John, "I will be staying overnight at my renter's farm." John stood listening to Joseph, but his mind was somewhere else. He was visualizing Rose alone at the cabin.

Joseph left the bank and so did John. John told his teller, "I'll be gone the rest of the day." He slipped out the back door, headed for the livery stable. He had his own horse in the stable. His buggy was sitting behind the stable. In a few minutes, John was on his way to see Rose. The trip usually took an hour. This trip took John thirty minutes. John pushed his horse to its limit. John stopped his buggy a short distance from the cabin.

Rose did not know John was there until she heard a knock on the door. Rose could hear Joseph's voice in her mind reiterating, "Do not open the door until you hear my voice." John knocked again and again. Each time he knocked louder. "Who is it, and what do you want?" she asked, from behind the bolted door.

"Rose, it's John Fitzpatrick. Please, I just want to talk to you. Joseph stopped at the bank and told me you were alone." She thought, that if Joseph had told John it must be all right. Rose was smiling as she opened the door. She had an unexplainable tingling inside of her. Rose was wearing overalls, a boys work shirt, and work boots. Rose wished she could have looked nicer, but after all, John had slipped out to see her without her knowing he was coming.

The instant Rose opened the door was all John had anticipated and hoped for. John was so excited. He thought she was prettier than he remembered. "Rose, do you remember me?" he asked. Rose put her hand out. John took her hand in his. He stood holding it, thinking how strong it felt. He felt the callus on her hand. This was the hand of someone who was not pampered, but who worked very hard.

John gently pulled her to him. Rose moved slowly, not knowing what was coming. His face was up against hers. He moved slowly, until his lips were on hers. The feeling was overwhelming. She had not been hugged, held close, or kissed, since her mother had died. Her arms went up around his neck. She had not ever felt this way before. Rose squeezed him so hard, it took his breath away.

When John released Rose, she felt weak and shaky. The need was there, the want was there, but the image of Joseph was everywhere. John told her that he had never forgotten her. He told her that he had thought of her often, and he told her how many times he had wanted to come see her.

Rose interrupted him, "We must never let Joseph know you were here. You must leave now." When John heard the desperation in her voice, he knew she was serious. "Please John," Rose begged, "Joseph would never forgive me. He is very possessive, and he will never let me go. John, you must go now." The urgency in her voice told him she would not betray Joseph.

It was twilight the following evening when Joseph arrived home. When he saw Rose, happiness showed all over his face. "I'm so glad to see you, Rose, I hope you were not afraid to be here all alone for the two days I was gone," Joseph blurted out.

"I was fine, Joseph, I read when I had my work done," Rose reluctantly told him. Her secret meeting with John Fitzpatrick was now buried deep in her heart, but the memory of his arms around her and the kisses they shared were so hard to forget. She found the only way to get John off of her mind was to work hard. Rose decided to go to the creek and do their weekly wash. She hoped this would also free her from the guilt she felt about lying to Joseph.

Chapter 14

Rose was at the creek washing clothes. She heard a noise that sounded like a woman moaning. She listened and heard it again. Rose walked quietly to the area. A young Indian woman was lying on the ground in the tall grass. Her hands were holding her swollen stomach. An Indian man was by her side looking bewildered and not knowing what to do to help. Rose approached them slowly, saying, "Please, let me help you. Please." She stood beside them for a minute to see how they would react to her. Rose kneeled down beside the woman and reached over and first touched her hand. Then, gently, she touched the young woman's stomach.

Rose could tell by the look in the girls eyes she was scared and in pain. Rose thought the girl needed a blanket to lay on instead of the hard ground. She also noticed that there was nothing in which to wrap the baby, once it was born.

Rose motioned toward the cabin and then motioned that she would return. Rose ran as fast as she could to the cabin. Rose could hardly speak. "Joseph, Joseph, I found a young Indian girl down by the creek having her baby. I need to help her! What should I do?" she asked. Rose continued, "She needs a blanket to lay on and a blanket for her baby."

Joseph said, "Rose, take the blankets you need. I'll put my pocketknife in the flame; you'll need to cut the baby's cord after you tie a small strip of clean cloth tightly around the cord. Wrap the baby in the blanket and hand it to the mother and step away. They need to be alone to share their love for their first born."

Rose returned with the blankets, knife, and cloth. Rose had only seen animals give birth, but she had read stories about the birth of a baby. Rose laid one of the blankets on the ground for the girl to lay on, then helped her to move onto it. The Osage Indian girl labored for hours. Rose went to the creek several times and wet a rag to wipe her off. She talked to her in a quiet voice, even knowing the girl could not understand her. Rose encouraged the Indian man to hold the girl's hand and rub the girl's forehead.

After the baby boy was born, Rose did what Joseph had told her. She took care of the baby's cord. She wrapped the baby in the other blanket and handed him to his mother. The Indian girl looked up at Rose and smiled. Rose stood up and walked to the creek bank with tears in her eyes, and hoped that someday she would know the feeling the young Indian girl was feeling right now.

Rose finished her chores and prepared supper for Joseph. She made enough to share with the Indian couple. She took the food down to them in one of her cast-iron skillets. She set it down beside them and left.

Rose was excited about seeing the baby the next morning. She left the cabin with breakfast for the couple and went to the area. Rose wanted to hold the baby. The blanket the Indian girl had lain on was there, folded up. The couple were gone. The blanket the baby had been wrapped in was also gone, because they had needed it.

Rose could not help the feeling of disappointment that came over her. She was thankful they had taken the blanket for the baby, because the day felt chilly. The leaves were turning yellow and dropping fast. The weather was changing again. Winter would soon come. This would be Rose's fourth winter with Joseph in the cabin.

ᴄ∽ Chapter 15 ᴄ∽

Rose knew that a trip into town would have to be made. She started another list. She had to plan enough food for a least five months, because Joseph could not make the trip if the weather was cold. Joseph's appetite was better, and he was enjoying his meals. He spent more time out of bed now. He would sit in his rocker in front of the fireplace and watch her work. Sometimes she would catch him staring at her.

This list was longer than the others had been. She needed a new pitchfork. The axe needed to be sharpened by the blacksmith. Rose asked for traps, because the creek was full of muskrat and beavers. She also had seen a lot of raccoons at night. Rose had learned how to trap from her father. He had always told her, "You are more skilled than I am."

She was hoping that by spring she would have furs for Joseph to take to town to sell. Rose hoped that he would bring her the money. If something happened to Joseph, what would she do without money? This trip was no different than the others. Rose got the team ready. She could hitch them and back them up as well as any man. Joseph left in the morning while it was warm. All the work was left for her to do.

That afternoon, Rose wrote about her life. She wrote about meeting John Fitzpatrick, and then about Joseph Higgins. She wrote and at times, it was almost unbearable. The afternoon seemed to fly by because of the chores she had to do. Darkness came with the night hours, and Joseph had not returned.

She began to worry. She wondered if it was over Joseph's safety, or because she would be homeless and very poor if something bad had happened to him. Rose had to admit that she was concerned about him, and did not sleep well that night.

It was midmorning when he returned. Joseph looked old and tired. He explained that John Fitzpatrick had told him, "You could freeze to death going home tonight. The temperature is dropping fast." Joseph had stayed in a room behind a bar. It had been so noisy that he had gotten very little sleep.

Joseph slept most of the day, while Rose unloaded the buckboard. The supplies would last until spring. Joseph woke for supper, and handed her the box he had secretly brought into the cabin. Rose pulled out a pair of long underwear. She wondered if he knew that she had been wearing a pair of his. Next she pulled out a pair of overalls, a boy's shirt, a couple of books, and a sack of candy. Tears welled up in her eyes. She had not had candy since she was a little girl. "Thank you, Joseph." He shyly smiled at her and nodded his head. Rose picked up one of the new books and started to read. Joseph laid on his bed looking at her until his eyes closed in sleep.

Winter was soon upon them in full force. Snow covered the ground. Joseph was able to carry wood into the cabin. He stacked wood on the porch so that it was close. Going out to the woodpile during the night was not safe, because the territory was full of wild animals.

Chapter 16

One night, Rose was leaving the barn after chores. It was clear, crisp, and very cold. She thought for an instant she heard a dog barking off in the distance. She closed the barn door and walked toward the cabin. Suddenly, the most ferocious looking dogs she had ever seen surrounded her. The hair on their bodies were standing straight up. Their mouths were open. Their lips were turned up, exposing long sharp teeth. They were extremely thin and mangy looking. One dog lunged at her. She felt his teeth tear at her leg. The next sound she heard was a shotgun blast and

one dog fell to the ground. The rest of the pack turned and ran.

Joseph hurried toward her. He saw that her pant leg was torn. He told her, "You need to wash the wound with lye soap and put horse salve on it." Rose wrapped her leg with the only slip she owned. He stood beside her while she dressed the wound. "The dog could have been sick. They never came this close before," Joseph said.

Joseph took care of her because he did not want to take her into town to the doctor. Rose tried to keep off her sore leg as much as she could. He helped her do chores the next few days, while her leg healed. She read books to Joseph during this time. After each book was read, Joseph would discuss the book with her.

He also told her more stories about the territory when the settlers first came. He told her how hard life was for them—clearing the land, building their log cabins, crops had been harvested with oxen or by hand. Women had to raise their families and also work in the fields with their husbands. The Indians roamed freely until homestead boundaries were set. Rose loved to hear his stories.

~ Chapter 17 ~

One day, she took Joseph to a special place she had found along the creek. Rose did not know why Joseph had told her about his land or why he said, "Be good to the tenants, they work so hard." Suddenly, the birds stopped singing. No sounds could be heard. Without any warning, six Indians appeared before them. They had found Rose's special place, Rose jumped to her feet. She stepped over in front of Joseph. The Indians were all looking at Rose's long blond hair. The Indian dressed as a chief rode up beside Rose. Joseph was yelling, "He wouldn't hurt you, Rose. He won't hurt you."

Rose stood very still, believing what Joseph had just said. The chief leaned over and touched her hair. He pulled on it. Then he sat up on his horse and spoke to the others. They all made a friendship gesture to Joseph, turned, and rode off. Rose remembered being very impatient until Joseph told her how he knew they would not be harmed.

Joseph told her of a cold rainstorm. He had been coming home from town with his supplies. He came upon two Indian boys huddled together along the trail. They were scared and cold, but also defiant. He stopped the team and stepped down off the buckboard. He carried his blanket and offered it to the boys. Joseph could see the fear in their eyes. The older boy had slowly reached out for the blanket, and put it around the younger boy. Through the use of Joseph's hands, the boys understood that he would not hurt them. He made motions to come with him to get warm and be fed.

The boys had stayed overnight. They lay on a blanket next to the fireplace. At daybreak, horses could be heard close to the cabin. Joseph opened the door, and the boys ran out to the man dressed as a chief, their father. The boys explained to their father in a foreign language why they had not returned home the night before and how Joseph had provided them with food and shelter. Without any common language, they formed a lifetime bond of friendship. Joseph allowed the Chief and his tribe to hunt and fish on his land though they could not go near any of the tenants or their cabins. Joseph was a very caring man who shared with others many times. Rose had been the one thing he would not share.

Chapter 18

One evening after they had eaten, Rose put another log on the fire. She chose the book she would read to him. With the fire crackling and with her reading aloud, she was surprised when Joseph sat straight up in bed. His arm came up.

He pointed to the cabin door, and then pointed to her bedroom door. Rose heard the loud pounding, and the loud voices that shouted to open the door, or they would kick it in.

Rose laid her book down and quickly went into her dark room. She closed the door and swiftly pulled her long hair up in a knot on top of her head. She grabbed her hat and pulled it down low over her forehead. She reached under her pillow for the revolver.

Joseph had to open the door. They were kicking it, and he knew they would break it down no matter what. The first man stepped in and pushed Joseph back until he stumbled. He grabbed a chair to keep from falling. The second man asked for his money and anything else of value. Joseph told them he only had a small amount. He had a leather pouch in his pocket with a few coins in it. He hardly got it out of his pocket when it was grabbed. The men wanted more. Joseph was hit in the face several times and then knocked to the floor. The strangers continued shouting and threatened to kill him.

Rose was terrified. She knew if they killed Joseph they would open her door and find her. She had to save Joseph now! Rose flung open her door and stepped out. She kept her head down and held the revolver aimed directly at them. She startled them. They all whirled around toward her. Rose said, "Leave my father alone and get out!"

Rose aimed the revolver at one of the men's boots. She pulled the trigger. She missed them on purpose. The bullet went through the floorboard. She raised the gun and said in a low voice, "The next one you get!" The three men hurried toward the door, swearing about the damn kid. They got on their horses. Rose stood on the porch, watching them ride toward town.

She went back in, locked the door, and helped Joseph up from the floor. Rose got a rag, dipped it in cold water, and gently cleaned the blood from his mouth. She lay him in his bed and covered him with his blanket. She laid another wet rag over his eyes. She knew that by morning his eyes would be swollen and black. How could anyone hit a helpless old man?

Rose could see he wanted to say something. But she told him, "We'll talk in the morning." Even with the pain, Rose thought he was smiling.

It was not until spring, when Joseph went into town, that he heard the story. The three rough, tough men had ridden into town and stopped to eat at the town's rooming house. Without knowing, they sat at a table next to the town's banker. They discussed that old man. He had more money. They just knew he did. If it weren't for that damn kid with the gun, they would have found it.

John Fitzpatrick knew exactly who they were talking about. John left the table and went to see the town Marshall. John told the Marshall that he needed to warn the three men to leave town, or they would be put in jail for breaking into Joseph's cabin. The three men had left town and rode in the opposite direction. John had walked back to his bank and thought about that kid. The three men never knew that Joseph had not told anyone about the break-in.

Chapter 19

The creek was thawed, and the trees were budding. Rose watched the muskrats splash in the water and thought about her twentieth birthday. Rose looked into the water and saw her reflection. She thought about something Joseph told her recently, "You have matured into the most beautiful woman I have ever seen." She had been living in the cabin with Joseph for over four years.

Rose had no bitter thoughts about her father any more. She had accepted her life with Joseph because he was a good, decent man. He had never been less than a gentleman. His life had been abruptly changed, like hers had been. He had done the best he could.

It was warm already at breakfast time. Joseph sat at the table while she had made him biscuits with eggs. Rose was aware of Joseph intently staring at her. She turned her head slightly, enough to see how he was staring. She went into the summer kitchen. When she returned, it appeared to her that his eyes were waiting for her to walk into the cabin. She knew he was watching her move back and forth from the stove to the table. "It would be so easy to love you, Rose," Joseph blurted unexpectedly. This was not what she thought he would say.

"Joseph, I love you too," she found herself responding. He blinked his eyes to hold back the tears, but he couldn't stop them. This love they felt for each other had grown out of a mutual need. They had been brought together by destiny, and Rose was a survivor.

It had been hot all day and was now beginning to cool off. Rose finished her chores early. Her mind drifted off, thinking about the water in the creek. She could go swimming, but that would leave Joseph alone in the cabin. He needed to get out too. It had been a good summer for Joseph. He got up frequently and walked outside. Rose moved his chair wherever he wanted to sit.

Rose went into the cabin, and casually mentioned what a good night for canoeing it would be. She knew that he had not been in his canoe for years. She went on to say how calm the water is, and that she would do the rowing. She told him, "I'd put a blanket and pillow down for you to sit on." Joseph sat looking

at her. He finally answered by saying, "Only a short trip." Rose clapped her hands. She made all the preparations. "Rose, you must bring your revolver, just in case." Joseph carried the lantern because the sun was going down.

They made a smooth entry into the water. Rose had the paddles and rowed the canoe toward her private inlet. The light made the water look as though it was dancing. The trees cast shadows on the water, which made it look mysterious. The beautiful wildflowers along the shore made the trip magical for them. Rose asked Joseph several times if he wanted to go back. "Not yet, Rose, please, just a little farther," he answered each time.

Rose did not want to tire Joseph so much that he couldn't walk back to the cabin. After Rose directed the canoe out of the water and up onto the bank in its usual place, she helped Joseph back to the cabin. The evening had been wonderful for them both.

⁓ Chapter 20 ⁓

At breakfast, Joseph mentioned a trip into town. At first she thought about asking if she could go along, but she said, "I'll make a list." Besides the food supplies on it, Rose added writing paper to the list. She had written in her log every day. She needed a pencil, garden seeds, and matches. She remembered something she had read about. It was called a hoe. She wrote it down without asking him. Two plates, two cups, and an oil tablecloth were added. Joseph read the list, folded it up, and stuck it in his overalls.

"Remember, Rose, do your chores early. Lock the cabin door, and open it only when you hear me call your name," Joseph firmly told her. While doing chores, Rose had always walked past the sleigh that Joseph had covered with a canvas. She had wished many times that she could use it. She thought that maybe next winter they could since Joseph was well again. Joseph returned before dark with all the supplies. The blacksmith had made her a hoe. He had also asked Joseph if he wanted a puppy, as someone had dropped it off.

While unloading the wagon she found a box for her. She now had a lamp for her room, new reading books, a comb, a hairbrush, and a mirror. In another box, which had a hole in it, was a little puppy. She gently picked the puppy out of the box and held it close to her chest while it wiggled and licked her face. Rose giggled and just held the puppy close.

Rose prepared their supper as usual. The puppy fell asleep across Joseph's lap, with its head across his arm. His hand held the puppy securely. At bedtime, Rose covered Joseph and started to read to him. He looked up at her and smiled. In a short time he closed his eyes in sleep. Rose leaned over and tenderly kissed Joseph on the forehead and said, "Goodnight, my dearest Joseph."

The puppy brought them both so much enjoyment. He was a constant companion to Rose. Rose decided to name him Pal, for he never left her side. Joseph sat on a chair outside and watched them. No one would ever come to the cabin again without warning.

Rose always remembered her twentieth birthday. Rose no longer minded when she remembered that she had not talked to anyone else but John and Joseph in four years. Her days went by so quickly with caring for Joseph, the chores, raising a garden, and taking care of Pal.

The books Joseph brought her to read were meant to help them both escape to places they would never go. But in their minds, they could see them.

The day was warm, and Rose wanted to get Joseph out of the cabin. She had found a wonderful spot on the bank of the creek. She took his chair and walked him slowly to the creek. She sat him down and covered his legs with a lap robe. Rose and Pal sat next to him on a gunnysack. Rose reached over and took his hand in hers. It was a time of peace and contentment for them both.

Joseph talked to Rose about the land he owned, the renters, and his respect for their hard work. He told her, "I hope that you will always be kind to others as you have been to me." He thought the time was right

to tell her. "They are drilling for oil in Oklahoma."
Rose wondered why he was telling her all of this.

Chapter 21

The summer of 1884 was hot and dangerously dry.
Rose was doing her chores one evening and suddenly,
she smelled smoke looked in all directions to see if she
could see smoke in the air. The smoke was coming
from the farm of one of Joseph's tenants. The wind was
blowing the smoke toward Joseph's cabin.

Rose ran to the cabin to inform Joseph. Harness
the horses Rose, I must go and help," he ordered her.

"Joseph, let me go help, too." Rose interrupted
him.

"No, Rose, you must stay here," his voice sound
harsh.

"Joseph, it's too dangerous for you to go alone, let
me help, too, please." Rose pleaded.

"No, Rose, get the wagon ready, fill the wagon
with the burlap bags stored in the grain shed. The
burlap bags will be soaked in the creek water and
hauled to the fire to beat it out," Joseph yelled at her
as she headed toward the corral.

Rose was angry while she harnessed his team. She
filled the wagon with the burlap bags, then brought
the team and wagon to the cabin porch. They were
both aware that the smell of smoke was getting stronger. They now could see the flames leaping into the
air. The wind was feeding the flames.

Joseph crawled up onto the buckboard. He turned
and told her, "Get to the creek and in the water, if

the fire gets here. If the fire gets to the oil, everything will burn." Rose stood and watched as Joseph headed in the direction of the horrifying fire. She knew this was a mistake. She was the one who should have gone to help. Joseph inhaled a lot of smoke before he got there. His throat felt raw, and his lungs were hurting when he took a deep breath.

Most of the townspeople came to help. People came from miles around, because the whole territory was dry. Everyone feared a fire. The women soaked the burlap bags in the water and filled the wagons. Joseph was one of the drivers taking the water-soaked bags to the fire area.

When John Fitzpatrick arrived, he demanded that Joseph help soak bags while he drove the team back and forth. John also took charge of each team from both running and inhaling the smoke. He would switch a team and wagon by taking the team out to rest.

John could see in places the underbrush had been laying for years. It was deep and dry. When it ignited, it sent the sparks leaping in the air. It was a raging wildfire. Suddenly, without warning, the wind that had been blowing fiercely in one direction turned. The fire started toward the homestead.

Everyone fought it hard, digging holes in the ground, and throwing dirt on the fire. The fire was out of control. The grain storage, chicken coop, and barn burned to the ground. They stood in stunned shock, feeling helpless, angry, and fearing that the cabin would burn next.

When John first realized the wind was changing, he ordered two of the wagons to go to the cabin and lay the wet burlap bags on the cabin roof. Sparks had blown toward the cabin, and it would have burned, but the sparks landed on top of the wet bags. The cabin and contents were saved.

When Joseph saw the fire burning the buildings, he worked until he was exhausted. John had been checking on him frequently. John found Joseph lying on the ground. Joseph had burns on his face and hands. Every breath Joseph took was painful, and he moaned. John knew that Joseph needed to be taken home. He picked Joseph up and put him in the buggy, while the renter drove Joseph's team home. They carried Joseph in and laid him on his bed. Joseph told them, "I'll be all right."

John knew that Rose was there, but that he was not allowed to see her. After John left the cabin, Rose tended to Joseph. He was black from his head to his feet. Rose was sure that the black soot would never come off with a wash cloth.

Rose was determined to get Joseph to the creek, to soak and clean his burns. She brought one of the horses up to the porch. She laid Joseph over the horse, and led the horse to a shallow area in the creek. Rose removed all of his clothes and put him in the water. She gently washed him with lye soap. Rose took Joseph back to the cabin and applied salve to all of the burn areas.

Rose told Joseph how she had watched the fire come close to his homestead, and how helpless she had felt. She went on to say, "The fire came right up to the creek, and because the creek was wide, the fire stopped." The remaining part of the summer and fall, Joseph spent most of his time overseeing the rebuilding of his renter's homestead.

❧ *Chapter 22* ❧

Winter started with a gentle snow. Joseph agreed that the evening was perfect for a sleigh ride. The moon was extremely bright, and it made the snow glisten. Rose hitched the horse between the shafts and led him up to the cabin. She went in and brought out the two pieces of iron that she had warmed by the fireplace, to keep Joseph's feet warm. Rose helped Joseph into the sleigh. She pulled the horse blanket over both of them. Joseph picked up the reins. He handed them to her and said, "Yes, you can do this."

Rose had not been this happy for a long time. She had learned to be content, but this made her extremely happy. She had been here over four years, and this was the first time Joseph had allowed her to leave his home. The ride was wonderful. She slowed the horse down to a walk. A feeling came over Rose that made her realize she had nothing to fear. She had done everything Joseph had expected of her since her arrival. And now, she felt secure. Just being with Joseph made her feel safe.

Joseph asked Rose to stop the horse. She pulled back on the reins, and the horse stopped. "Rose, would you leave me if you could?" Joseph asked.

Without any hesitation, Rose looked right at him and said, "Joseph, I will never leave you."

"When I made the decision to send for help, I asked for an older woman to take care of me. You, Rose, came instead. Everything I asked you to do has been done right. You are the most important person in my life," Joseph confided. Joseph wanted Rose to see his land. He directed her, but they stayed away from the tenant's homestead, for of course, he wanted no one to see her. Rose belonged to him, and he dearly loved her.

It was a good winter for sleigh rides. Rose took him on quite a few. It was as though they were the only two people in the world. What they didn't know was that they had been seen on one of the rides. After chores and breakfast one morning, Joseph told Rose that he had asked John Fitzpatrick to come to the cabin. He did not tell her why.

Rose tried to hide how she had reacted to hearing this. She immediately visualized the kisses she and John shared that day, when he had unexpectedly came to the cabin when Joseph was not there. Her stomach felt a little upset. Her face was flushed, and she said, "I need to bring some food from the cave if he stays for dinner." Rose needed to get out of the cabin to get some fresh air. Rose wanted to change her clothes. She wanted to put on the new dress Joseph had bought her when she first came here, but Joseph must never know her feelings for John.

Rose had prepared their dinner, when she heard a knock at the door. Joseph went to let John in. The two men shook hands, and then Joseph turned and said, "John, do you remember Rose?" Rose felt like she was standing in the black sticky liquid. Her feet would not move. John walked to her. He took her hand in his and politely said, "Of course I remember Rose."

Standing there looking at each other, it was as though they were all alone. Suddenly, their thoughts were interrupted by the sound of Joseph's voice saying, "Rose has dinner ready, and we will eat before we talk." Joseph began by telling John about Rose's love for books. He said, "She reads to me every day. She has made me well again." He continued, explaining how Rose did all the chores while he was ill. How she carried the water from the creek. John knew now how much Joseph loved Rose. He also knew that he had to continue hiding his feelings he had for her.

After dinner, Rose said, "I have something I need to do outside."

John thanked her for dinner, and told her, "It was very good." Rose stayed out of the cabin until she saw John leave in his buggy. When Rose entered the cabin, after she had completed her chores, she found that Joseph had set the table for supper. The lamp was lit. Rose noticed what a good mood he was in. John had told Joseph that one of his tenants had come into the bank and asked who Joseph had living with him in the cabin. John's answer had been that he did not know.

Chapter 23

The tenant had eaten dinner at the rooming house, and had told the story to several people in town. Two young men working at the livery stable heard the story. The young men had seen Joseph come into town for supplies, but had always seen him alone. They thought they'd take a ride out to Joseph's just to see. Without telling anyone they were going, they rode out of town just before dark.

Joseph was in the cabin, with the lamp lit. He was putting more wood in the fireplace. Rose would fix supper when she finished her chores. The young men rode up to the cabin. They rode their horses right up on the porch. Pal was with Rose, so Joseph was not warned of the intruders.

He heard snorting from the horses. Joseph opened his door in disgust. The horses were right in his face. Joseph thought they were going to ride into his cabin on their horses.

Joseph was so frightened he could hardly speak. One young man said, "We want to see who you have living with you."

"I'm alone! I live alone," Joseph told them. Joseph knew Rose was doing her chores, but he did not know how soon she would be done.

The men backed their horses up and told Joseph they were going to search all of the barns. Joseph turned and quickly went to his gun box. He pulled out his shotgun. The young men rode their horses to the barn and looked all over. One man walked through the barn. The two young scoundrels looked into every building, and no one was found. They rode back to the cabin and told Joseph they would be back. Joseph was so angry. He was so relieved when they left without finding Rose.

Rose had taken one of the horses to the creek to water. While she was there, she had heard horses whinnying. She knew someone was at the cabin. Pal heard the noise too, but Rose grabbed him and held him close to her chest for he wanted to bark. Rose remained there in the dark until she knew the visitors had left. She worried about Joseph, and she did not know if she had done the right thing.

Joseph's eyes were full of tears when he saw Rose enter the cabin with Pal. Rose could see the sense of relief on his face. Joseph stayed extra close to Rose the rest of the winter. He did not tell her he feared that the young scoundrels would return.

The next morning Joseph asked Rose if she needed anything from town. He had decided he needed to go. "No, Joseph, you can't go that far in this chilly weather. You could get pneumonia. I'm going to refuse to harness the horses for you," she told him. He promised her he would dress warmly. He said, "I'll do my business, and I'll hurry back." He was planning to see the Sheriff. He was going to tell the sheriff that if the two young men ever came to his cabin again, they would be shot. Rose tried to get him to wait a few weeks for the weather to get warmer. Joseph flatly refused.

Chapter 24

Winter was nearly over when Joseph told Rose he had not been feeling well. She had heard him coughing during the night. In the morning she had been putting a pan of water on the fireplace since the air in the cabin was so dry. Rose thought that must be what was making him cough. Joseph asked her to make a mixture and lay it on his chest. It was a remedy his mother had used for colds when he was young. She cooked oatmeal, spooned it into a cloth, and laid it on his chest.

Rose begged Joseph many times to let her get the doctor. He always refused. Rose had been with Joseph five years, and she knew she had given him a love that he had never had: one of companionship, kindness, and compassion. The kisses they shared were when she finished reading to him. She would kiss his forehead. Rose was the love of his life.

Joseph was very sick now, and Rose's life was about to change. Rose was doing all she could to make him comfortable. She fed him meals while he lay in his bed. She would sit beside him, holding his hand, and read to him for hours. Joseph continued to cough, and she noticed that he was spitting up blood. Rose wished she could do more for him.

Rose thought about her mother, and how ill she had been before she had died, and about the days they had spent together. Rose had sat by her mother's bed and read to her. Now she found that she was doing it all over again, for someone else she loved very much. She remembered everything that her mother had told her. She had instructed Rose about the dress she wanted to be buried in. Rose had been asked to wash it and have it ready.

Rose's thoughts came back to Joseph. She would have to find something for him to wear. The tears came so easily lately. Pal lay by his bed, and at times he would sit up and lay his head next to Joseph's. Rose continued to ask if she could take him into town to see a doctor. He answered by saying, "You can take me to town when the time is right."

Joseph's condition was getting worse each day and in a whisper he said, "If anything happens to me, go into town and get John Fitzpatrick right away." Besides doing her chores, Rose sat by his bed most of the day. Joseph was dying, and she knew it.

Joseph died early on a spring morning in 1885. She laid her head on his chest and cried like her heart had been broken. Rose left the cabin with Pal at her side. She hitched up the horses, and she and Pal went into town to tell John Fitzpatrick. Rose cried all the way to town. She pulled the team slowly up to the hitching post in front of the bank. Her eyes were red. Her hair

was wind blown. She walked into the bank with Pal at her side.

John immediately stood up. He walked to her, knowing that something was wrong. Even in Rose's sadness, John thought she was beautiful. It was hard for Rose to say what she had come to tell him. Finally, she said, "Joseph has died, and now I'm all alone." John told her he would take care of everything as Joseph had instructed him to. Joseph had told him to help Rose if something happened to him.

Joseph would be buried next to his father and mother, on his land. Rose told John she only had a small amount of money, gained from the furs she had trapped. She thought she would go back to St. Louis and live with her father. John stood for a long time looking at Rose. She didn't know. Rose did not know that she was now one of the richest women in Oklahoma.

John got all the papers out, including the deed. He laid them in front of her, and said, "All of Joseph's land, money, oil, and one half of the bank are all yours." Rose sat for a long time before she could say a word. Then she began to cry. Sobs came uncontrolled. She began to question herself. Did she deserve this? In five years, she had gone from being penniless to being independently wealthy.

When Joseph's body was removed from the cabin, a letter was found addressed to Rose. He had put it under his pillow before he died. Rose did not open it until after the funeral. Pal lay at her feet and she read it out loud. It began,

"My beautiful Rose, when I opened the cabin door five years ago and a frightened little girl stood looking at me, I had no idea you would give me five of the most wonderful years of my life. You turned out to be the kindest and sweetest human being I have ever met. No one else gave me the joy that you did. When I realized that I loved you, a day did not go by that I didn't wish I were young again, because then I would have asked you to marry me. I could not bring myself to share you with anyone else.

"At times I did not thank you for all the work you did. No one else would have done it, and you never complained. I love you even now, as you read this. I could not give you anything in life, so I'm giving you everything I have in death. The land, money, oil, and the bank are all yours, to do with as you wish." Love, Joseph.

If only she could ask Joseph whether it was alright for her to accept all of this. She had depended on him for five of the most important years of her life. Rose spent a month alone in the cabin. She was grieving and mourning the loss of someone such as herself, someone that had sacrificed his life. In the month alone she decided to spend her life helping others, people less fortunate than she was now.

⟨ Chapter 25 ⟩

John Fitzpatrick pulled his buggy up in front of the cabin. He knocked on the door.

As Rose opened the door, he stepped in and set his briefcase down and reached for her. He pulled her tightly into his arms. She put her arms around his neck, and the kiss they shared told her that he loved her, too. Her future was changing again. Rose needed to make a trip to St. Louis, for she had forgiven her father. Rose knew John would be waiting for her when she returned.

When Rose boarded the train for St. Louis, she was wearing a black satin dress. Her black coat was ankle length and had a fur collar up around her neck. Her black boots were laced with leather strings. She wore a large rimmed hat with a black ribbon around it. The black ribbon was tied in a bow in the back. On her shoulder hung an expensive black leather satchel with her initials imprinted on it.

A few strands of her blond hair hung softly around her neck. She looked like a picture.

Minutes earlier, John had stood holding her to him. He pulled her soft body to his. John's hand had moved down her back and pulled her to him. His mouth had opened and he put his lips on hers. John wanted her now, and he would share her with no one. John Fitzpatrick stood and watched Rose board the train. He had kissed her again and said, "Rose, I love you, and I will be waiting for you."

As the train pulled out, John thought back to five years ago. He had stood right here and watched a young girl get off the train. She had been wearing a large coat and worn-out gloves. The shoes she had worn were scuffed and looked too big for her. But John remembered thinking she was so beautiful. John had taken her to Joseph. He remembered that when he had pulled up in front of Joseph's cabin, he had wanted to turn his buggy around and take Rose back to town.

John had known that he couldn't do that; Rose had been sold to Joseph. Rose's father had promised her to Joseph Higgins for fifty dollars. John wondered if Rose knew about the money. He knew she had forgiven her father for sending her to Oklahoma. Did she know about the money exchange?

The noise of the train made Rose sleepy. She removed her hat and leaned her head back to rest. Her memories of Joseph flooded her mind, and sadness overcame her. Joseph had needed her. As bad as it was at first, she had been needed. Rose missed feeling needed.

The tenant nearest to the cabin had taken Rose's livestock to his farm while she was gone. He was also taking care of Pal for her. She missed him, too.

Rose's eyes were closed, but her mind would not rest. Rose kept asking herself, "Did I do everything I could have for Joseph?" On the day she had arrived five years ago, and Joseph had gotten out of bed, he had struggled to get to the door because he could hardly stand. The sores on his head had been infected, and flies in the cabin were landing on his head. Rose had tried to do everything she could to heal his sores and make him well. She thought about how tired she had been the first week she was there. Joseph had depended on her for nearly two years. After he had gotten well again, Rose had depended on him.

Rose had often wondered why it had been John Fitzpatrick who'd met her at the station five years ago. It was not until Rose visited the bank after Joseph's death, that John had explained, "The bank belonged to Joseph and me," he said.

When the town had settled there, Joseph had opened the bank with John's father. When John's father died, John inherited his father's share. Joseph had once told Rose he had worked in the bank before his father had sent for him. What he hadn't told her was that he owned one half of the bank. Now, the bank belonged to her and John.

⤳ Chapter 26 ⤳

It was dark outside now. Rose awoke with a start. She reached into her satchel, and her hand felt the revolver. Rose had promised Joseph that she would never travel without it.

Joseph had left Rose with many memories. The dress he had bought her at the general store was the one she had worn to his burial. He had told the clerk that the dress was to be sent to a relative who had hit upon hard times. Since all the clothes Joseph had bought from the general store in the last five years were all smaller-sized men's clothing, no one ever suspected she was with Joseph.

The day of Joseph's burial was warm, and Rose had not needed a coat. The only coat she owned was the one her mother had made, and her only coat was all worn out. When Rose had pulled the team to a stop at the gravesite, she had noticed that the tenant farmers and their families were all there. Most of the people who lived in town had also been there. Standing in a semi-circle in the back was the whole Indian tribe.

Slowly, a young Indian girl had ridden her horse up beside Rose. Sitting in front of his mother, astride the horse, was a small Indian boy. The young mother handed Rose the blanket Rose had given her a few years before. The young mother pointed to her son and said, "Jo, Jo." Rose remembered thinking if only Joseph could see this now.

The train was pulling into a station, where Rose needed to change trains. She looked so beautiful that everyone turned to look at her. Rose boarded the new train. The conductor was calling, "Next stop, St. Louis." She looked and found a vacant seat where she could be alone.

Rose noticed a man in a dark suit. It reminded her of the suit she had buried Joseph in. She had found the suit all folded up in a box, one he had worn when he worked in the bank many years ago. Rose had taken the suit and laid it on the porch railing to air out. She had no money at this time to buy a new one, it would have to do. With tears in her eyes, Rose remembered the last thing she had done for Joseph. She had trimmed his hair and shaved him before going into town to talk to John Fitzpatrick.

As the train was slowing down, Rose's thoughts were interrupted by the conductor saying, "Next stop, St. Louis." Rose stepped down from the train with her satchel. She walked to the livery stable. She asked to rent a horse and buggy for two days.

It was dusk now. She knew that if she hurried, she could get home before dark. After the short trip, she pulled the horse to a stop in front of the gate, tied up the horse, and walked slowly to the door. Rose could see light from a lamp coming through the window. Rose knocked on the door. It took several minutes, but the door slowly opened. Rose looked into her father's eyes. He said, "Emma? Emma, is that you?"

"No, Father, it's Rose. Mother died ten years ago, " Rose answered.

"Rose, I'm almost blind. You look just like your mother. I can't believe you're here, " he said.

"Why did you come here now, after what I did?" he inquired ashamedly.

"I came, Father, to tell you I forgive you, and to ask you why." she responded.

Rose stood quietly listening and watching her father. She had remembered her father as man who stood tall and straight. Now, he was stooped and bent forward. She noticed that he was looking in her direction, but his eyes were closed. His hair was gray now. She didn't remember her father having gray hair.

Louis Donlin began by saying, "Rose, I will always regret what I did. I did the worst thing any father could ever do. I have prayed for you every day since you left. I do not know how you can ever forgive me. I hoped that the man I sent you to took good care of you. I prayed you had a nice home, with lace curtains on the windows, and good food to eat. I prayed that he provided well for you. I never wanted to hurt you in any way. The money I received...," her father started to say.

"The money you received!" Rose became angry instantly. She repeated what her father had said. Rose's voice cracked, and she asked again, "Joseph

Rose's Betrayal and Survival

sent you money for me?" Tears were running down Rose's cheeks. "What was I worth, father? How much did Joseph pay you?" she cried.

Louis Donlin turned and reached out his hand for the back of his chair to steady himself. He dropped into his chair. He was feeling remorse and ashamed. He put his head down, but Rose could see his tears. The only time Rose had ever seen her father cry was when her mother had died. Rose was determined to find the reason a father could sell his only daughter, "Why Father? Why?" Rose continued to pressure him.

Her father wiped away his tears. He began by telling her, "Soon after your mother died, I noticed I could not see the traps as I could before." He paused. "As time went by, I could not get the traps set. I thought if I could not trap, how could I buy supplies? How could I take care of you? The day I read the notice in the general store, I was not trying to get rid of you, Rose. I wanted to find a good home, with a husband to love you."

"Oh, Father," Rose said. She wanted to tell him about Joseph. The words would not come. Her father had been hurt, too. Louis realized that Rose was extremely tired from her trip. He insisted on taking the horse to his corral. He told her that he had memorized the homestead. Rose walked into her bedroom. She stood and looked at it for a long time. She lay down on her childhood bed, and for a moment it was as though she had never been gone.

Rose could hear thunder, and then the sky lit up. Suddenly, rain was hitting against her windows. She remembered the rainstorms at the cabin the first year she was there. The roof had leaked all over. She had set pots and bowls on the floor because the cabin would have water all over the floor otherwise. The rain had dripped down on their beds, and Rose had moved their beds frequently.

Patching Joseph's roof had not been an easy task for her. Rose had found boards to cover all the leaks. She used the team and wagon, first putting the boards in the wagon. She had driven around the cabin, throwing the boards up on the roof. Rose had used the seat of the buckboard to climb up on the roof. It had taken several rainstorms before all the leaks were stopped.

Rose lay in her bed and thought about the last five years. She closed her eyes, and Joseph's face appeared. He was smiling and saying, "Rose, remember to be good to everyone. Help anyone who needs it. The money you have is a large amount."

Rose walked into her father's kitchen the following morning. He had breakfast all ready. The table was set. Rose's bowl was set in the same place it had been when she was growing up. Her father greeted her warmly like he had done each morning while her mother was alive. When they sat down to eat, Rose began, "Father, I would like to take you to Oklahoma City to see an eye doctor."

"I can't do that, Rose, I have no money to pay a doctor," he explained.

"Father, I can take care of everything for you. Please, Father, come with me," she pleaded. Rose knew her father was feeling unworthy of any help she could provide for him. But she would insist.

Rose felt that the opportunity Joseph had given her was about to start. She decided never to look back at the bad things that happened in her past. Rose wanted to let Joseph live through her. She would never let Joseph Higgins be forgotten. He could have done great things for the state of Oklahoma. She would do it for him.

Joseph had prepared her for a life of dedication and service to others. One of the things Rose thought about for a long time was building a library. Joseph had always bought books for Rose, because he could afford them. Rose knew that the settlers, and parents with large families, could not buy books for their children. With a library, all children could take a book home to read, and then bring the book back. This was a dream she was destined to live out.

Another dream Rose had was to build a hospital. She had often thought about the Indian girl and how she had laid on the ground to have her baby. Rose felt that no woman should ever have to deliver her baby in the grass, and that women should have clean beds to lay on. Rose would train midwives to deliver babies.

The new library and hospital would have Joseph Higgins' name in large letters on the front of each building. Joseph's cabin would not be lived in, ever again. Rose was going to build a new cabin on the edge of town, which she hoped someday she and John Fitzpatrick would live in as man and wife.

In the last five years, Rose had watched more oil seep up onto Joseph's land. Joseph had told her that the time was right to drill for oil. She would see that the drilling began after her father's eyes were taken care of.

The long path that Louis Donlin had set out for his daughter had taken many turns. He had wanted only the best for Rose. Now, Rose Donlin had the best.

For additional copies of this or other
books written by Phyllis Collmann:
phyllisacollmann@hotmail.com
1-712-540-4082
www.collmannwarehouse.com